Meet the BOBS AND Tweets

by **PEPPER SPRINGFIELD**

illustrated by **KRISTY CALDWELL**

SCHOLASTIC INC.

Dedicated to Raisa and Mort with love
–PS

For Pepper. You are 50 percent Bob,
50 percent Tweet, and 100 percent fabulous
–KC

Library of Congress Cataloging-in-Publication Data available

ISBN 978-0-545-87072-6

10 9 8 7 6 5 4 3 2 1   16 17 18 19 20

Printed in the U.S.A.   88
First edition, July 2016

Book design by Becky James

TABLE OF CONTENTS

CHAPTER 1
A MOB OF BOBS

A mob of Bobs lives like slobs.
A mob!
Of Bobs!
Oh, such slobs.

Seven Bobs are in the mob.

Can you see that six are slobs?

Bobs yell. They burp. Bobs howl. They fight.

Their pit bull, Chopper, snores all night.

These seven Bobs, they have to move.
Their neighbors *do not like* their groove.
So what will be the best address
For a mob of Bobs who makes a mess?

This mob of Bobs, they call up Mo.
"Hey, Mo! We hear that you will know
Where we, who are a mob of Bobs,
Can find a house near other slobs."

"Bobs, pack up your van," says Mo.
"I *know* where you need to go.
19 Bonefish Street for you!
Trrrust me, Bobs, my word is true."

The Bobs yell, "Whoop! Whoop! Just show us the way.
We are set to go. We will leave today.
We trust you, Mo, that you know best,
That Bonefish Street will pass the test

And be the very best address
For Bobs like us, who make a mess."

"Whoop! Whoop!" cheer the Bobs as they pull into their lot.
"We are here: Number 19, the Bobs' new hot spot.
Our house is perfecto—outrageously good.
Bobs love Mo for finding this new neighborhood."

They unpack the Bob van. They hang out their sneakers.
They unload their guitars, their drums, and their speakers.
"Let's play some music! Let's have a food fight!
On Bonefish Street, Bobs can party all night."

But Little Bob Seven is looking around.
He does not hear anyone making a sound.
I am worried, he thinks, *about all my Bobs.*
Is Bonefish Street really the place for such slobs?

CHAPTER 2
A FLEET OF TWEETS

Now meet the Tweets.

A fleet of Tweets.

Of seven Tweets, just six are neat.

Tweet One

Tweet Two

Tweet Three

Tweet Four

Tweet Five

Tweet Six

And then one more . . .

(She would be Tweet Seven.)

Please greet this fleet of cleaning Tweets.
Tweets love to wash. Tweets wipe their feet.
Tweets do not yell. They are quite polite.
Their cat, Pretty Kitty, purrs all night.

This fleet of Tweets, who are so neat,
They want to find a brand-new street
Where they can do their cleaning jobs
Far, far away from any slobs.

This fleet of Tweets, they call up Mo.
"Mo! Is it true that you will know
Where we, who love to be so neat,
Can find a home just right for Tweets?"

"Tweets, sweet Tweets, my name is Mo.
Yes! I know where you should go.
Bonefish Street is right for you.
Trrrust me, Tweets, my word is true."

The Tweets pack up their things so neat.
They ride to 20 Bonefish Street.
They sing sweet songs and talk in rhyme
And find Tweet ways to pass the time.

"Yippee-yee!" peep the Tweets. "We made it at last!
That long trip on our bikes went by pretty fast.
Mo was right! This is a neat-lover's place.
Hurry! Let's fix up our brand-new Tweet space."

Tweets unpack boxes. They pick out their rooms.
They start dusting and mopping and sweeping with brooms.
But Little Tweet Seven refuses to clean.
She just wants to read her new cat magazine.

So she pitches a tent and turns on her light.
Then what does she see? A huge, rowdy food fight!
"Hey, look, Pretty Kitty," she says to her cat.
"Do you think we should tell our Tweets about *that*?"

CHAPTER 3
BOB SEVEN

Six Bobs are food fighting and singing real loud.
Bob Seven goes upstairs, away from the crowd.
He unpacks his clothes and his books and his toys.
He wears his new headphones to block out the noise.

You see, Little Bob Seven is not like the mob.
He is not, he is not, he is *not* a big slob.
He is very careful. He likes to be clean.
He likes to be liked, and he never is mean.

He cleans up his room, and he washes his plate.
He likes to be early. He hates to be late.
He uses a napkin. He is always polite.
He does not make noise if it is late at night.

He loves each of the Bobs—Bob One through Bob Six—
But he knows he does not quite fit in their mix.

CHAPTER 4
TWEET SEVEN

Tweet Seven will not clean. She is off on her own.

She plays a new video game on her phone.

She has not unpacked. She did not make her bed.

But she taught Pretty Kitty to stand on her head.

You see, Little Tweet Seven hates to be clean.
She will never go near a washing machine.
She plays in the dirt. She gets awfully messy.
She does not like anything fancy or dressy.

She slurps chocolate Blurpees and loves rock 'n' roll.
In each one of her socks is a *verrrry* large hole.
She does not like dusting. She will not use a broom.
She heaps piles and piles of junk in her room.

She loves each of the Tweets—Tweet One through Tweet Six—
But she knows she does not quite fit in their mix.

CHAPTER 5
SIX SWIMMING TWEETS

The Tweets wake very early to greet the new day.
They eat a good breakfast, put their dishes away.
The Tweets all do sit-ups till their tummies are sore,
Then on to do yoga, downward dog on the floor.

The Tweets have been cleaning all morning since dawn.
They clean up their rooms, then they trim their new lawn.
They make a new sign so bold and so clear:

At noon, Tweet One says, "Come on, Tweets, let's swim!
We have to work hard to stay healthy and trim.
We will go to the pool and swim one hundred laps.
We will wear our new wet suits and brand-new swim caps.

Chopper rolls 'round on the Tweets' lawn so green,
Right in broad daylight where he can be seen.
Bob Seven reads the sign so bold and so clear:

PLEASE KEEP
OFF THE GRASS!
THE TWEETS NOW
LIVE HERE!

"No, Chopper, no! Come back to me!
Quick, let's get home before anyone sees.
I have a bad feeling this is not too good.
Neat Tweets live here in our new neighborhood."

"Come on!" Bob One shouts. "Let's go! Let's get moving!
We are off to the pool for splashing and grooving.
Let's load up our Jet Ski™. Come on, let's get cool.
Time for Bob fun at the Bonefish Street Pool!"

The Bob van is filled—it is totally packed
With sandbags in front, a red Jet Ski in back.
"Come on now, Bob Seven, put your hat on. Let's roll!
And *puh-leese* untie Chopper right now from that pole."

The Bobs drive to the pool. They back their van in.
"Whoop! Whoop! We are here! Let the Bob bash begin.
This is awesome. Perfecto! Outrageously good.
We are glad to be here in our new neighborhood."

Bobs fire up the grill and crank up the tunes.
With huge bags of sand, they make huge sand dunes.
Bob Seven keeps Chopper away from this scene.
He puts on their life vests and lots of sunscreen.

The Bobs drive their Jet Ski right into the pool.

"Whoop! Whoop!" yell six Bobs. "This is really so cool."

"Hey," says Bob Four. "Hey, you Bobs, look at me.

Check out my handstand on one water ski."

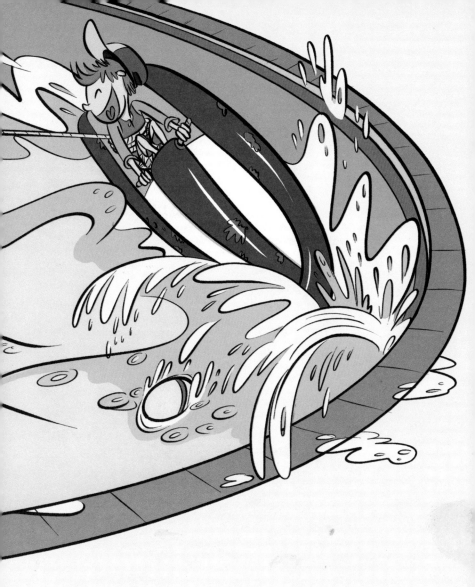

Six Tweets are still swimming their one hundred laps.
You can just see the tops of their brand-new swim caps.
Then, uh-oh, the Tweets, they are swamped by the boat.
All six swimming Tweets, they cannot stay afloat.

CHAPTER 7
BRAWL AT THE POOL

And then the brawl starts! You can imagine the fight.
The Tweets peep quite firmly, "You do not have the right.
You cannot drive a Jet Ski that way in the pool."
"But why not?" yell six Bobs. "We do not see a rule."

"This pool is for swimmers who live on our street.
A nice, safe, cool spot for We-Who-Are-Neat."
"*Not!*" yell the Bobs. "We do not think so! *No way!*
This pool is a great place for Slobs-Hard-At-Play."

Bob Seven tries hard to stay out of the way.
He makes up a ball game that Chopper can play.
But his aim is not good. He cannot really throw.
He is never quite sure where the big ball will go.

Pretty Kitty floats on her pet water bed.
Bob Seven throws and just misses her head.
Chopper runs for the ball, trying to fetch.
Tweet Seven jumps up and makes one great catch.

Pretty Kitty gets wet and lets out a loud howl.

"So sorry," says Bob Seven. "Here is a dry towel."

"Hey," says Tweet Seven, "my name is Lou."

"Hello," says the boy. "It is nice to meet you."

"My name is Dean, and I live with those Bobs,
But I am different. I am not a slob.
I read in the shade. I like to stay clean.
I am a regular kid, if you know what I mean.

"We Bobs had to move—we got kicked out of our place.
The neighbors did not want such slobs in their space.
Mo told us that this is the best place for slobs.
She said Bonefish Street rocks for a mob full of Bobs."

"Oh, boy!" says Tweet Seven. "I bet it is true . . .
Mo made the same promise to us and to you.
'*Trrrust* me! *Trrrust* me! *Trrrust* me,' said Mo.
'Bonefish Street is where neat Tweets need to go.'

"We Tweets rode our bikes a very long way.
From morning to midnight, we rode the whole day.
We came here to Bonefish Street, Mo told us to.
She said, 'It is perfect for neat Tweets like you!'"

"That Mo," says Bob Seven. "She lied to us all.
And now she has caused a huge Bonefish Street brawl.
Look at those Bobs and those Tweets in the pool.
They are yelling and fighting. This is not cool."

"Let's go," says Dean Bob. "Enough is enough.
This brawl in the pool is getting too rough.
Let's go find the lifeguard to break up this fight.
Knowing my Bobs, this could go on all night."

CHAPTER 8
HELP!

So Chopper and Dean and Pretty Kitty and Lou
Walk over to the lifeguard and call up, "Hey, you!
Our Bobs and our Tweets are having a fight.
You are the lifeguard. Please make it all right."

"Okay," says the lifeguard. "My name is Mark.
I swim like a goldfish. I hunt like a shark.
I have lifeguard training in breaking up brawls.
Give me a minute while I make a few calls."

"*No way,*" says Lou Tweet. "Put down your phone!
We kids cannot handle this brawl on our own."
"Hurry!" pleads Dean. "Come down from your chair.
You cannot help Lou or help me from up there."

Lifeguard Mark gets down from his tall lifeguard chair.

He takes out his whistle. He combs his long hair.

He lets out a shout as he strides to the pool:

"You Bobs and you Tweets, I have made a new rule!

"On the left of the rope, the pool is for slobs.

That is where you should go, all of you Bobs.

To the right of this rope, the pool must stay neat.

That is the best place to swim if you are a Tweet."

"Lifeguard Mark," says Bob Seven, "your plan will work fine.

My Bobs can be slobs to the left of your line.

They can play Marco Polo and make lots of noise.

They can splash all they want with their loud water toys."

"Lifeguard Mark," says Tweet Seven, "I like how you think.
To the right of this rope my Tweets will not sink.
My Tweets can swim laps and do water ballet
With all of those noisy slobs out of their way."

"Okay," says Mark. "That is it. No more brawls.
Now I am going to make my phone calls."
"Lifeguard Mark," says Dean Bob, "you saved us. Hooray!
Now at last Lou and I, we can go play."

"You rock, Mark," says Lou, "your work here is done.
Now Dean and I can have real kid fun."

CHAPTER 9
FRIENDS

"Phew," says Dean Bob. "I am glad Mark helped out.
I get really stressed when my Bobs start to shout."
"I agree," says Lou Tweet. "I am glad Mark came through.
Most of all I am happy I got to meet you.

"I have been trying and trying and trying all day
To stand on my hands, but I just seem to sway.
I need someone with me to help hold my feet.
Will you help me, Dean Bob?" asks the littlest Tweet.

"Of course!" says Dean Bob. "I would love to do that.
Let me tighten my life vest and take off my hat.
The kiddie pool is a good place for your trick.
I know if we practice, your handstand will stick."

Lou practices handstands. Dean holds her feet.
Then they go to the snack bar to get something to eat.
They order burgers with ketchup and crinkle-cut fries.
"And two Blurpees," says Lou. "The extra-extra-large size."

Later, Dean says, "Let's go sit in the shade.
I want to show you some drawings of Chopper I made.
Plus, I have a new book I think you will like
About a cat who can dance and ride on a bike."

At four thirty Bob One says, "Come on, Dean, let's go!
We have to get home to watch a new TV show.
We will eat Sloppy Joes—a Bob-o-licious Bob dinner,
Then race our new go-karts to see who is the winner.

"We will play midnight football, and wear our new cleats.
And forget that our pool fun was spoiled by Tweets."

"Come on," peeps Tweet One. "Lou, go get your bike.
We have to get home for our pre-dinner hike.

"We will use what we learned in our group trekking class,
Then come home for supper of raw kale and fresh bass.
We will practice deep breathing to work off the stress
Of those horrible Bobs who made such a mess."

"Midnight football?" asks Lou. "Your Bobs stay up late!
My six Tweets get tucked in no later than eight."
"I know," says Dean Bob. "It is never too good
When my Bobs all move in to a new neighborhood."

So Lou Tweet and Dean Bob say their good-byes
As Chopper eats up the last of the fries.
"Let's play tomorrow," Lou says to Dean.
"I can come pick you up at Number 19."

"Yes!" says Dean Bob. "I will meet you at eight.
Do not ring the doorbell—my Bobs all sleep late.
I am happy, Lou, that you are my friend.
I will see you tomorrow. Good-bye now."

THE END

What's next?
BOBS AND Tweets
Perfecto Pet Show

COMING SOON!